To my **Little Bush Girl** K.,
stay wild, always!

I was born in a cabin in the Canadian Northwest.
The winters were cold with sticky snow, but our home was
cozy, and we enjoyed a simple life.

The wilderness was unforgiving. There was a fast and cold river that ran near our cabin. Even though it brought us fish, my parents never allowed me to go there on my own. The bears liked to hang out by the river anyway. The snow on top of the mountains in the middle of July reminded me that winter never really left this beautiful place. My parents called me Kaani. Although I was just a small girl, they already knew I was a wild child. I was as strong-willed as they come.

We had two puppies and my dad's dog. They were my only friends, until my little brother came along, which suited me well.

I could roll around in the grass, drink from puddles, and chase squirrels with them. Their tails wagged frantically. They were always ready for an adventure.

I remember waiting for Dad by the windowsill, a steaming cup of tea in my hands. He would come back, walking in the dark because the days are extremely short in the deep of winter.

His dog pulled the sleigh that carried the day's catch—often martens and the odd lynx.

Mom would later skin the animals, put the furs out to dry, and cook their meat for our dogs. When Mom had finished tanning the furs,

she would sew them into warm mittens, hats and soles for our boots. Then, she sold the rest of the pelts for food and supplies later in the season.

When my little brother could sit up on his own, Mom took us with her to set snares along the river. It was my first introduction to dog sledding. Mom bundled us in a caribou skin. Often, my other travel companions might be a frozen rabbit or two lying across my legs. Little Brother was very curious about the rabbits. Together we looked for their tracks and trails in the snow. So, Mom quickly turned our fun into our job, and we loved it. Despite the temperatures that froze our wide river and all the lakes on the land, checking the snares became my favourite time of day.

The following winter, the puppies were old enough to pull the big sleigh. It took us farther into the bush, so my dad didn't have to walk the long trail anymore. It was a dark and narrow path that led deep into the forest.

Dad was glad he could travel it faster. At first, the dogs played, fought, or just lay around, getting tangled in the harnesses my mom had worked so hard to make. Dad was not impressed.

But when I ran in front of them, they sprang forward and followed me. It was just another game for the dogs while I had to run in my heavy snow boots.

After teaching them a few times, they started doing what they were supposed to do. Then there was no stopping them.

With my dad on the long trail and us on the river, we just didn't have enough dogs, especially since my brother and I were getting bigger. In the spring, we had puppies again, and I was over the moon! Altogether, we now had seven dogs. When they were big enough, Mom had a surprise for me. The best surprise yet. She told me I was old enough to have my own dog team!

Of course, this meant a lot of responsibilities and some skills I had to perfect, but I was overjoyed. I was now mainly responsible for one female dog, Mooney, soon to become the leader of my team, and one male, Volto, that would do most of the pulling. He was called the wheel dog and stood right in front of the sleigh.

I had to start the game all over again. Running ahead in the wet snow of November, I took them on longer and longer walks. I taught them when to stop or go, when to go left or right. Some days I got discouraged, while others were plain fun.

After all, my dogs didn't have an older dog to show them what to do. Eventually, they learned to love how fast they could run on the frozen river, our own giant race track, barking and whining when I stopped to check a snare.

I often came home with wild stories to tell Dad, tricks I had learned with my dogs, and things I had seen on the land. One time, the dogs spotted a moose on the trail and ran so fast to catch up to it that I lost my hat! They only stopped when the snow got too deep for them. The moose didn't mind it though.

I told my parents that I was going to be the best musher in all the North one day, and I would win all kinds of races with my dogs.

Printed in Great Britain
by Amazon